THE REST DIE TOMORROW - ASCENSION

First edition. April 2, 2022.

Copyright © 2022 Julius St. Clair.

ISBN: 979-8215500903

Written by Julius St. Clair.

Also by Julius St. Clair

Angelic Testament
End of Angels
Angels of Eden
Angels and the Ark

Depression Series
Depression Vol 1

Fantasy World Earth Anthology
Fantasy World Earth Anthology Vol 1
Fantasy World Earth Anthology Vol 2

Fantasy World Naropa Anthology
Fantasy World: Naropa Anthology Vol 1
Fantasy World: Naropa Anthology Vol 2
Fantasy World: Naropa Anthology Vol 3

Fantasy World: The Explorers
Fantasy World
Fantasy World Vol 2 - Expedition One
Fantasy World Vol 3 - The Protectors
Fantasy World Vol 5 - Utopia

Julius St Clair Short Stories
Sanctuary (A Short Love Story)
My Best Friend is a Killer: Short Story Collection
World War Baby: Day One
World War Baby: Day Two
Static Rain
Girl of My Dreams
Face Punch
Face Punch II: Two for Flinching
Champion: Reluctant Hero
Champion #2: Family Reunion
Champion #3: Broken Promises
The Weather Brothers
The Weather Brothers #2: Fighting Immortals
The Weather Brothers Vs Champion
The First and Last Kiss

Sage Saga
The Last of the Sages
The Sage Academy (Book 1.5 of the Sage Saga)
The Dark Kingdom
Hail to the Queen

Of Heroes and Villains
The Legendary Warrior
The End of the Fantasy
Rise of the Sages
Ancient Knights
The Last War
The End of an Era
Hail to the King
The King's Apprentice
The Legend of the Sages

Sage Saga Bundle
The Sage Saga: The Complete Five Kingdoms Trilogy
The Sage Saga: The Complete Bastion Trilogy
The Sage Saga: The Complete Sorcerers Trilogy
The Sage Saga: The Complete Time Travel Trilogy

Sage Saga Collection
The Complete Sage Saga Collection
The Complete Sage Saga Collection Vol 2

Sage Saga Duologies
The Last of the Sages Book 1 and 2
The Last of the Sages Book 3 and 4
The Last of the Sages Book 5 and 6
The Last of the Sages Book 7 and 8
The Last of the Sages Book 9 and 10
The Last of the Sages Book 11 and 12

Seven Sorcerers Saga
The Sorcerer's Ring
The Sorcerer's Dragon
The Sorcerer's Blade
The Complete Seven Sorcerers Trilogy

The Rest Die Tomorrow Miniseries
The Rest Die Tomorrow - Ascension
The Rest Die Tomorrow - Judgment
The Rest Die Tomorrow - Killbox
The Rest Die Tomorrow - Endgame
The Rest Die Tomorrow: The Complete Collection
Shepherd of the Wolves

Wishes
A Wish for Love and Vengeance
A Wish for Us

Witchfall
The Harvest
The Blood Witch

Standalone
My Immortal Playlist

The Last of the Guardians
The End of Us

Table of Contents

The Rest Die Tomorrow - Ascension (The Rest Die Tomorrow Miniseries, #1) 1

PROLOGUE 3

CHAPTER 1: GROWING PAINS 6

CHAPTER 2: STILLBIRTH 20

CHAPTER 3: TRAINING 33

CHAPTER 4: SERENITY [Day 0/8]{Dec 24th – 10 A.M}........ 48

The Rest Die Tomorrow
By
Julius St. Clair

PART 1 – ASCENSION

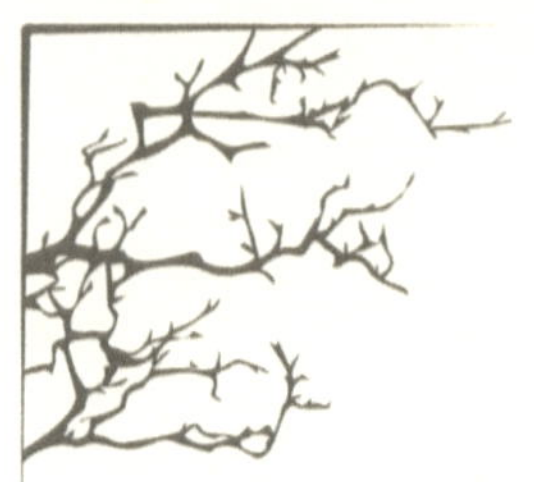

PROLOGUE

"Ladies and Gentlemen, to best sum up the man we are commemorating, it is appropriate at this time to discuss his character first...and upon great reflection, I can give no better caricature than this portrait, painted through his own words: 'Even if I end up in Hell...I will have all of eternity to outsmart the Devil.'

He proudly spoke these words in the midst of adversity, and they are a perfect picture of who Vincent really is. Arrogant, selfish, narcissistic – these are not traits worthy of honor and respect. As it stands, we are continually struggling to remove those of similar qualities from our leadership positions and political offices. Far too many of our very own children idolize men of this caliber and invest their futures in practices that destroy our society every day...

"So, you may ask, why are we here? Why is this despicable man worthy of our attention? Because, without him...many of us would not be here today. In a time when our world needed change and revolution, but we were too lethargic to take a stand, he decided to do it himself. And if you knew Vincent like I did, then you understood that when he said something, he meant it, and unlike many others, he had the ability to back up his words. This was a dangerous man, who could have easily exploited our hard labor for himself. But he sought out a legacy, one to leave behind when he would die, and this dream, despite its selfish intentions...saved us all.

"He was tested and attacked on all sides, but today we are the results of his ordeal. Results that reveal that no matter how one is perceived, it is only a snapshot of the album that is one's life, and Vincent, with all of his contemptible attributes, still had a heart. Is this man worthy of our respect? Does he deserve to be remembered? Allow me to expound further on the subject, and I'll let you be the judge..."

From a speech given by Katherine Alexander at the 35th annual Think-Emergence Convention

CHAPTER 1:
GROWING PAINS

No one is born evil. It is a slow cook, a dish bred of a chef's lack of attention. It takes time to become the man people are disgusted with, the monster they pray they will never become. I wish you could just turn off who you are like a machine – press a button and immediately you're not tempted by all the forbidden things people don't like to admit they enjoy, like money and power. But life isn't that simple.

I tried simple once. After all, it was my security blanket for the first thirteen years of my life. But at each rite of passage, every step toward adulthood, the blanket began to tear and degrade. Back then I still believed in the world like Santa Claus – jolly, fat, full of opportunities... I never really saw any danger, my head always found buried in my books and not in the game. If I had been more vigilant, maybe my life would have taken a more appropriate turn. I could've become a fireman, or an astronaut – any number of jobs that kids dream about when they're young.

But I wasn't attentive, and I didn't see him coming at all – a disturbed and malevolent classmate of mine who decided to force his way into my humanity and refashion me to his liking. I tried to hold on, preserve my innocence as long as I could, but no one can keep a grip on what they love forever, and eventually I had to let go, and wake up to reality.

"Vincent, wake up!" she shrieked, slamming the palms of her hands onto my desk, her massive wedding ring creating an unnecessary knocking sound that made me wince.

"I told you the answer was fifty-seven," I said coolly, turning my gaze back toward the windows. Of course I had not said anything prior, but with the right answer plowing through her ears, any comeback she had was now void and forgotten.

"That doesn't mean you weren't daydreaming just now," she accused me correctly. I wanted to do many things to her right then, all of them unacceptable by my school's code of conduct, but I maintained my composure and once again donned the cloak of the ignorant child.

"You're right, Mrs. Larson," I replied believably. "I should have been paying attention. The only reason I knew the answer was because I went ahead in the workbook. It's no excuse really. I'll start listening."

She rose from my personal bubble with a smug look on her face as I returned her authority and power willfully. I could see the forgiveness on her lips before she even spoke.

"It's okay to daydream, but there is a time and place for everything. You're in school to get an education, which won't magically appear when you decide to grow up and pay attention. Look outside."

I obeyed, for the sunshine dancing and glittering amongst the leaves was so much more inviting than my academic prison.

"The time you put in now will pay off later. Just because you want to make a million dollars and be like those famous rappers all you kids are into these days, doesn't mean you will. It takes hard work that many of you are not accustomed to."

By now, my classmates were staring at me intensely as if I were a lab specimen while Mrs. Larson was yammering on and on about the economy and self-entitlement. Jason, two seats diagonally to my right was shaking his head in amusement, a silly smirk developing with the full intention of making me laugh. I bared my teeth at him inconspicuously, letting him know I wanted him to stop and he shrugged his shoulders in response. I didn't want to chuckle and get into further trouble.

"Don't worry. She's gone," he mouthed silently, making the universal sign of insanity toward his right temple.

Gone she was, for now she was throwing her hands into the air, walking back to the front of the classroom where she had now transitioned from teacher to preacher, bringing down the fire and brimstone while we were berated for simply being children. I allowed myself to look around the room, ignoring the forty desks that crowded most of the space or the dirty blackboard that had been stained to the point we could barely read anything from it. The unswept floor, the lonely walls, the donated outdated technology – these were all too familiar and common for their existence to hold any weight in my thoughts, so I turned to my classmates. One caught my attention in particular, sitting a seat diagonally to my left.

He was a joke to the whole "made in the image of God theory," having a visage that resembled a pit bull's and repulsively dirty blonde hair - rustled and untamed, aimlessly reaching to the sky in all directions. His skin brutishly complemented his colossal frame which was aged beyond its years. His eyes were listless and dark, and his very presence was foreboding.

Why he was staring at me at that moment, I could not know, but I was determined to find out.

"What?" I snapped at him, giving it my best tough guy voice. He didn't move. I wish I had known his name, but I was generally oblivious to the quiet ones so I never made an effort to learn about them. Apparently he knew mine though.

"Vincent," he stated emotionlessly as he continued his passive assault.

"What do you want? Why are you staring at me like that?"

He began to stare at my shoes and then slowly looked me up and down, almost seductively, sending a chill up my back. He licked his lips absent-mindedly and went back to gazing into my eyes. At this point, my entire being was quaking and I couldn't keep up my tough guy mask much longer. Jason had noticed the unwanted exchange between us by now and threw down his desk to get Mrs. Larson's attention. The crash startled everyone including me, and when I looked up to see if the predator was still staring at me, he had already turned around in his desk and was facing ahead. Jason gave me a worried look while the kids laughed at how scared Mrs. Larson had been.

I paid no attention to them as I assessed the situation. What was that kid's problem? I didn't think I'd ever said a word to him in my life so why was he making it a point to single me out? Maybe Jason knew who he was. I'd ask him at lunch privately.

The bell for lunch rang suddenly as Mrs. Larson glared at the clock. Looks like today's lesson would have to wait for tomorrow. I grabbed my backpack before I realized it and rushed to Jason. I refused to look back at the kid who had stared me down earlier, but I could feel his eyes on me.

"Let's get out of here," Jason said, looking behind my shoulder. He didn't have to say anything for me to know what was wrong.

Navigating the halls of our cramped little high school was like going white water rafting. Sure it was fun at times, especially when you got to see your friends between each period, but mostly it was tiring work that required quick reflexes and inhuman strength...if you wanted to keep your head anyways. Fortunately for me, Jason was a professional that pushed the "rocks" out of our path with relative ease. I shadowed him precisely, trying not to give him a flat tire until we finally made it outside where the kids who were done with their lunch (or never got it to begin with) hung out, laughing and discussing the usual topics of conversation like which singer had the better album or whether the Steelers could win this year with the starting quarterback being injured. Jason instinctively went to our usual spot, a picnic bench close to the cafeteria doors. Many people preferred privacy and congregated in the back so our chosen bench was always available. Jason collapsed on the bench and sighed into his hands, rubbing his forehead vigorously.

"What did you do to piss him off?" he groaned to me as I threw my hands in the air.

"Are you serious? I didn't do anything! One minute me and Mrs. Larson are talking and the next, he's staring at me like a creep. Who is that guy anyway?"

"You don't know who that is? Where have you been in the last year?"

"Why? Should I be worried?"

"His name is Donald Harrison—"

"-well now I understand why he's mad, but I still didn't name him."

"Can I finish? This Donald guy, I don't know why you're on his radar all of a sudden, but you need to get off. He's a real upstanding guy. Already he's put two kids in the hospital because all he wants is some attention from his negligent father. You remember Brian? Tall, lanky kid who's always wearing those corduroys? Donald put him in the hospital a couple weeks ago because he bumped into him in the hallway. That's who we're dealing with here."

"See, Jason. This is what I'm talking about," I sighed, exasperated. "That's the whole point of our company. Our company will put an end to people like him."

"What company?" he asked, genuinely confused.

"Don't tell me you forgot already."

"Oh, you mean Eclosion? C'mon, admit it. It's a stupid name for a company."

"That's our company you're insulting right now, and maybe Donald is coming after me because he knows what our company would do. People like him wouldn't be able to hurt anyone again."

"What does Eclosion even mean?"

"Can you get off the name already? That's not the point."

"Tell me what it means again and I'll move on."

"It's the emergence of an adult insect from its shell, like a butterfly emerging from its cocoon. I chose the name because anyone who joins us will not be a larva anymore. They will rise into their full potential and come out like a butterfly."

Silence.

"That may have been the dorkiest, stupidest thing I've heard in my entire life."

"C'mon, Jason. It makes sense though, right?"

"I can't be going around telling people what you just said. Seriously I can't. Why did I agree to this again?"

"Because you see it all around you. The injustice of it all. Think about all those kids that are beaten up and taken advantage of, while the bad ones get a free pass in life. We're just trying to even the scales. Make things the way they're supposed to be."

"How does this all work? Remind me," he groaned, rubbing his forehead and closing his eyes.

"We pretend to be a profitable business, like selling T-shirts or lemonade—"

"-lemonade?"

"-yes, okay, selling something, but it's all a front. Secretly, everyone that's a part of our 'company' will really be together to stop the injustice going on in our school, and later when we get bigger, we'll change society."

"Soooooooooo, we're trying to be like crime fighters, superheroes?"

Jason looked around him to see if anyone was listening. Thankfully, the student body was too busy throwing burnt pizza and soggy nachos at one another.

"No, not exact...okay kinda. It's all inside job stuff. We earn a reputation as being an upstanding successful business, but it's just a way to get people to meet and revolutionize. We can use our individual talents to change things. In our meetings, we will discuss how."

"Why all the faking? It sounds like a lot of work. Why don't we meet out in the open and people know we're protesting and stuff?"

"Because people in power hate change, especially when they want to stay on top. The principal would disband us, or people would be too scared to join us openly. We have to be secretive. This Donald character probably found out from some of the recruits that our first plan is to get all the 'bullies' expelled from school."

"Honestly, I think you're being a little paranoid, but I see your point. Like, we can't just get the school together and say we are all demanding he gets expelled. That would never work openly."

"Not to mention Donald would go on a rampage while we're doing it. Besides, I like people being happy, at peace. I don't mind us doing the dirty work behind the scenes. Eclosion will work. We just need a few more people before we carry this 'expulsion' plan out."

"Okay, but can we at least think about changing the name? We have time. It's not like we know if all this planning is going to work out yet."

"It will. In the meantime, I'll try to stay away from Donald as much as possible. He might just be acting weird, but if he really knows about our expulsion plan, then he's targeting me for a reason."

"What are you going to do if you can't avoid him?"

"I don't know. I'm not going to lie and say I'm not scared, but when I started this whole thing, I knew the risks. I have to keep going...who knows, maybe if he tries to touch me, I can fight back and get him expelled."

"That won't happen. He'll just be suspended and so will you."

"Maybe I can...no, that won't work..."

"What?"

"I thought maybe I can...take him out permanently...but it's a ridiculous thought."

"Yeah," Jason glared at me, "because that's murder."

"That's why I said it wouldn't work. I could never go through with it. I'm just trying to figure out what will stop him. I don't want to just get beat up and that's it."

"Yeah, but we're not even thinking about killing someone. Don't take this Eclosion thing too far. It's fine we're all secretive and stuff, but we're doing this clean. Let's go through with our expulsion plan and be done with it. He doesn't deserve to die because his parents can't raise their child right. If he comes after you, you run, and that's final."

"You're the one who asked. I didn't think you'd get so angry."

"I didn't think my best friend was suggesting murdering someone."

The air was a little awkward after that, and I couldn't help wondering what Jason thought of me. Sometimes I was too logical for my own good. Of course, I couldn't kill someone. I knew it was wrong, and it would make me worse than Donald. At least he only sent people to the emergency room, and not the morgue. But deep down, I knew that if the expulsion plan didn't work, and he found out who was responsible for the attempt, we would all be in trouble. He didn't seem like the type that would hit it and quit it. All of his victims so far were innocent bystanders but he would have a legitimate reason to come after us. We had to be prepared for the worst.

Jason glared at me one last time as the bell rang for us to go back to class. I was still hungry, but I could wait until after school. Jason often did the same and his mom usually made the best second lunches for him consisting of a spread of steaks, roasted potatoes and corn on the cob. Just thinking about it made my mouth water and I knew that whatever he thought of me, I had to rectify the situation before school was over. I couldn't go to my house. Most of the time my mother was working her two jobs while my father, the lazy drunken bum that he was, would take it upon himself to eat whatever I had made for myself, telling me he needed the energy to "lead". What a joke.

"So, based on the fact you didn't eat your free lunch, I'd say you want to come over after school?" Jason said flatly, reading my mind.

My stomach growled in response. Jason laughed heartily and patted my shoulder. We were friends again.

"No hard feelings, man. You can come over, and we can talk more about this company of yours with the horrible name."

I nodded as now that one problem had been resolved, I could worry about the other. I had to avoid Donald as much as possible until I figured out a desirable solution, but with class in the way, I would barely have time to think. And there was no telling if Donald would suddenly appear before the end of the day. I needed a plan, or I would have no clue of how to react if he confronted me.

"Hey, Vincent. Wake up," Jason said, snapping his fingers in my face. "We only got three minutes left. You know you can't be late for math again."

"I'm not going today," I said authoritatively. Jason gave a "seriously?" look and then quickly looked back at the swarm of students disappearing back into the school.

"And where are you going?"

"To think, maybe read. I'll be by the old willow tree up the hill."

"Which reminds me. I heard Donald also hangs out with the Willow Tree Street gang. Thought you should know."

"Is that tree up on the hill their turf?"

"No. Their gang is named after the street they live on, but I'm just saying, be careful. They're a new gang but they have a reputation of being ruthless."

"What kind of a gang names themselves after a street? What if one of them moves?"

"Who knows? So, you coming?"

"No."

"So what if Donald is out here stalking you? Aren't you safer inside?"

"No one goes by the willow tree. I'll be safe."

"For such a non-risk taker, you sure are playing it dangerous."

"He can find me in the building. He has no clue where I am outside of it."

That seemed to be good enough for Jason, who was already wondering what the teacher might say to his football coach if he was tardy.

"Alright, Vincent. Be careful. I'll see you at the end of the day."

"I'll be there," I assured him as he ran like a cheetah through the double doors, back into the school. I made my move before any of the teachers or custodians saw me, taking the latest thriller novel by Ernest Harper and clutching it like a necklace to my chest. It was an insane psychological ride about a man who discovered he was thinking with someone else's brain. I don't even know how that works. I mean, how would you know when you are you? If you get the original brain back, will you have the same thoughts? Or are you suddenly a different person with no clue something changed? I was poised to find out.

Making my way to the willow tree was as simple as breathing for I had done it so many times in the past. Even in middle school, I had often skipped a meaningless subject or two to migrate over to the high school's mascot. It was something about the way the branches shaded you from the world which appealed to me. I had never been a religious person, but this was truly my sanctuary, the only cathedral that could bring me into a state of internal worship and meditation. I was at ease here, and no one ever bothered me. Until today.

I had been careless, letting my novel absorb me to the point all my senses became numb. I didn't hear his heavy breathing, his awkward steps, and before I realized that someone was near, I found myself staring into the face of destiny.

He didn't care that I was inferior in stature; he just needed someone to take his rage out on. It was all over his face and pouring from his eyes. I tried to reason with him, if only to delay whatever plan he had devised for me personally.

"Are you here because of Eclosion?" I asked him cautiously, my voice low and meek.

"No," he said. "I don't know who that is."

The fact that he said "who" and not "what" said it all. He had no clue what I was planning with Jason. So why was he here? Why was he bothering me, who gave nothing to the world but silence and indifference? I asked him so.

"I don't like the way you look," he said, grinning devilishly at the end of his articulate speech. Really? Was that all? I was just "his next victim" and nothing more? The cover of my paperback was beginning to get damp from perspiration, my vision blurring from the salt water. Where was Jason when I needed him now? Why did I take a chance and skip class?

If this moment had happened in my more recent years, I would've expediently introduced his face to the pavement and called it a day, but I was too pretty back then. Moisturizer with promised aloe was still a second layer of my skin. My clothes were yet to be more than cashmere, and I was still afraid to get dirty, afraid of my clothes shrinking in the wash, afraid of confrontation - but I was a faithful believer in the theatrical.

Films told me schoolyard bullies lacked confidence, that they were cowards to aspiring heroes. They told me I would win because I was "good" on the inside, that as long as a shred of compassion existed, Lady Justice would flip the bill. All I had to do was stand tall and fight him head on.

But as I stood up from the base of my school's old willow tree, leaving my pleasure reading to the side, I couldn't help but wonder if they were silent witnesses to the upcoming slaughter. The wind was already unforgiving and nipped at the joints in my body, but that was the price of reading in solitude, especially in a time when books were an endangered species. The hunters sought out the precious life, assimilating old friends into their doctrine – a belief that reading was unnecessary and that those who did such were of a socially dying breed.

With each grade I moved on to, young readers learned how to lose the sheep's clothing and don the coat of the wolf, but I held onto my books like a child to his mother's leg. I was determined to remain true to myself and not change like the rest of them did. If my outcast reputation was the reason I was being targeted, then I had to prove him, just this once – that I was not to be underestimated.

I stood my ground as the bully grunted something inaudible, as expected – sluggard to the bitter end. I tried to be tough and reminded him of where his father was, or rather – wasn't, and he didn't like that too much. He said how he'd been watching me for some time now. I questioned his sexual orientation, and suddenly, I was on the ground, nursing the left side of my jaw.

His right fist, clenched in fury, calloused and worn like leather, was slow – a perfect symbol of his character, but my body refused to move. Was this what it was like to be in shock? I vaguely remember the smell of stale cafeteria hamburgers coming from the school kitchen, the taste of blood as my teeth held onto my lower lip; the surge of adrenaline igniting a flame through my veins...but I do not recall his fist connecting.

The pain was memorable though. The mini-explosion that was shocking and all too real, breaking all assumptions that I could deal with his onslaught based solely on will. The frozen grass crunched between my opening and closing fists as I writhed like a helpless worm after the rain. I longed for rescue but none came, for that specific tree I chose for reading was nothing less than a wall between me and the insignificant school I attended down the hill. My thoughts became his own as he realized how close we were to the building, and for a moment, he stopped to assess his surroundings. Seeing no consequence for his actions, he promptly capitalized on my weakness, the now familiar hurt exploding like mines all over my body as he willed them into existence with brutal, savage strength.

I tried begging. I pleaded. I let reason and logic, my old friends, speak on my behalf. I gave him options that were better than punching me into the ground. I told him what the consequences were for beating up a fellow student. But it was to no avail, and soon even reason vanished, leaving my attacker to do his will without contest. I cried for help, with all the fervency of a newborn baby, hoping that maybe Jason would suddenly appear, coming to check on me again, but there would be no salvation. I was all alone. My body being destroyed as well as my self-esteem and my pride...until something finally answered, and it rose from within.

Hate was its name.

I had met it before, but not formally. It was the type of creature to stand outside your house and wait to be let in. No knocks, rings of the doorbell, but I knew whenever he would arrive – his presence foreboding and intimidating, confident I was peering at him through the peephole. Usually I tried my best to ignore him, but this time I was ready to embrace his help. He played no games with me. He simply demanded for me to let him take control.

I did.

I threw honor to the wind and instinctively went for the coup de grace. I had been told to never go for a low blow on a man, yet I learned it was the only option for one of such a small frame like me. The bully yelped like a wounded animal and immediately this Rottweiler lost its teeth. He almost fell to the inviting underbrush, but humiliation caught his buckling legs. It didn't matter as my hands lunged toward his body, coursing with a new kind of poison. My fingernails became venomous fangs – my right fist striking with all the power and resolve to swallow my prey whole. Lashing out instinctively, furiously, blindly – he didn't feel like a rock anymore. His grunts began sounding more and more like a soft whimper – until an involuntary cough escaped his chest and snapped me out of my attack. A heavy silence blanketed our metaphoric boxing ring. No one had witnessed my triumph, but I didn't care. Finally, I could go back to my books. I had time now...

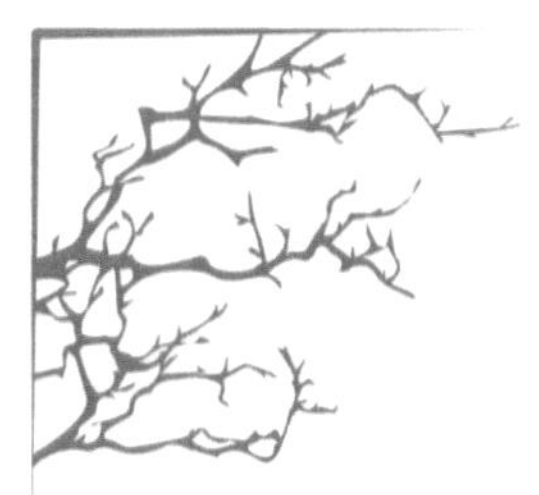

CHAPTER 2:
STILLBIRTH

They told me I had beaten him to a pulp. I wasn't sure what the phrase meant exactly, but ironically, I suddenly had a craving for orange juice. I received none, but the school administration took the liberty of calling my parents. The infamous ride to the police station was both surreal and anticlimactic. The officers sat in front of the wire frame that intentionally separated good from evil, whispering about how dangerous I was, to inflict such damage to another human being – their assumptions, convicting me before I had said a word. No one had asked for my side of the story when I was found behind the weeping willow. I guess my predator had spoken quite adequately in his silence, for I was promptly snatched away from my reading and held until the police arrived. The minimum wage politician I knew as my history teacher kept a steady hand on my shoulder the entire time, staring at me with righteous indignation, his "A" student now a hoodlum – one of them.

And so, I was taken to the station, where class skippers, gang members, and borderline rapists were interrogated and sent on their merry way – given a fifth, sixth – infinite number of chances to clean up their lives while I would not be afforded the same. I was expected to understand the rules of society and follow them accordingly. Supposedly, I knew better, while my classmates were sick in the head, confused, or had had a difficult childhood; therefore, a chance to strike again was allowed. I didn't know they changed the rules of baseball...

I wasn't obese, but the chair kissed my thighs all the same. The curved metal back support braced against me so hard, I thought I had scoliosis.

The room was as lonely and frigid as a mountaintop – the grainy gray walls enhancing the stale, thin air; the numbing cold clinging like wet jeans to my bones. The only reprieves were a one-way mirror, which may as well have been a wall, and a table to rest my arms on.

One of the officers who took me in broke protocol and started questioning me without my parents' consent. He was a stereotypical cop – one of the overweight, righteous kinds that spoke to me like I was a drug lord. I let him get out his frustrations, for I had already resolved not to speak. I had to tread carefully. It wasn't every day you saw a teenager engrossed in a novel next to a crimson mound of unidentifiable flesh.

"You know you almost beat that kid half to death?" he spat in my face, which was the worst interrogation tactic as of yet. I stifled a laugh, but he caught it before it dissipated.

"You're sick, son," he said through grit teeth. "But don't worry, we have a specialist coming in just for you."

I shifted my listless eyes to the right, staring through the concrete walls. Maybe he was right. Maybe I was sick. I felt...different, and I doubted it was the puberty. Before, my composition could best be described as one of fear with a pinch of anxiety, but now, I sensed an incalculable change that scared me to no end. It was like I didn't feel anymore, and I couldn't know what the consequences of such a loss could be. Hate had overtaken my heart and I refused to let go. Hate was now my mentor, my mother and father – my friend. Only hate had saved me – not them. When I needed Jason most, he was in class. When I needed a teacher to pass by, they were too busy. Sure, it could easily be said that the whole predicament was my fault. If I had went inside, Donald wouldn't have found me. But like the damsel in distress, I cared little for the reputation and past of my savior. I embraced him in my arms and cried onto his neck with gratitude. For so long I had tried to avoid conflict, minding my own business and skating through life. But it seemed fate had other plans for me, as if it wanted me to take a more active role for some unknown purpose – what that purpose was, only time would tell. But instead of expressing my thoughts, I played the humanity card.

"Is he okay?" I asked, my voice sounding natural and full of concern.

"He's in a coma," the officer said flatly, looking at me credulously.

"I hope he recovers," I lied, surprising myself on how easily it slipped out.

"Of course you do," he said between grit teeth, turning his head to a noise behind him.

The only door to the room slammed opened with authority as three adults entered. Two of them I knew all too well.

"What have you done?" the woman cried, with chestnut-colored hair covering half of her face, her eyes frantic and worried. She was unsure of what emotion to trust – fear of the charges against me, or concern, perpetuated by motherly instinct. I noticed that, despite the urgency of the situation, she still managed to end up arriving here in her most expensive attire. Gaudy jewelry and makeup were applied with the precision of a surgeon, and it cloaked her like royalty. The older man was stoic, his favorite gray wool suit jacket comfortably draped over his shoulders, the khaki shorts he wore only on special occasions gracing us all. The police officer halted his interrogation at the appearance of my father – that husky, serious man...but it was only because he didn't know him for the sponge he really was. My father tried desperately to be a rock, but the slightest bit of emotion invoked an outpour of monsoon quality that his wife regularly had to clean up the best she could – only for him to pretend as if nothing had happened. They disgusted and inspired me at the same time, for it was because of my parents that I worked hard enough to achieve greatness in my academics – if for no other reasons than to ensure that I would not become like them. Someday I would leave their care and never look back.

The third adult was a mystery man with a foreign air to him, his look matching the vibes he gave off. His oasis eyes and sandy skin were just as odd as his lanky, skeleton-like frame. He wore a three-piece suit and his glasses were rectangular and smooth, a perfect symmetry to his boxy and angular face. His composure suggested a strive for perfection with a hint of established superiority. Ignoring my mother's words, he extended a bony hand that immaculately complemented his fake smile. I was scared to grab it. It might break on me.

"Vincent, it is nice to meet you," he said. "My name is Dominic."

"Who are you?" I inquired. "Really."

This mystery man intrigued me, for although I wasn't a stranger to diversity, I had never seen a human being that looked so exotic and unique. Instantly, I forgot my parents were in the same room.

"Now, Vincent," he said condescendingly, "I already told you."

"You know what I meant."

The command in my voice tingled across my skin, catching me off guard and relaying a startled expression upon my face. Dominic ignored it.

"Of course I know," he smiled. "Well, to put it lightly, I am the leading practitioner of child psychology and deviant behavior in the state. We specialize in diagnosing children with special needs. You may be a candidate if your test results deem you so."

"So, a kid gets beat up on school grounds and you get a call? That's interesting. Where were you two weeks ago when Donald nearly killed a classmate of mine? Did you call Donald in then? Huh? What are you going to do to me now? Put me on an IEP and call it a day? WHAT-"

"-VINCENT!!!" my mother shrieked, standing up and slamming her palms onto the table. "Don't you talk to an adult like that! You know better!"

I turned to my creator in defiance, boring a hole through the very eyes that could once subdue me. She gasped in astonishment and clung to my father's arm. He was unaware of his wife's plight, staring at the adjacent wall, locked in a daze.

"No worries, Mrs. Alexander," Dominic stated assuredly. "It is vital that he speaks his mind. Besides, I am perfectly in control."

Oh. Is he now?

"But he knows better," she lamented, pleading with the man to condone her outburst.

"Be that as it may, you must allow me to conduct the conversation. We spoke about this earlier in the vestibule."

"He's not a bad boy," she continued, ignoring him. "I don't understand why we're here - he couldn't have done what you claim. How could he have hurt that boy? All he does is read silently and keep to himself. He's been in fights with other children in the past and this has never happened. If anything, he's always the one to come home bruised and swollen."

"Everyone has a breaking point, Mrs. Alexander."

"But he has perfect grades in school. He's a good boy. I don't see the problem."

"His teachers seem to have a different interpretation. They say he's variant, always countering what they say with his opinion when he called upon – he talks out of turn, sometimes disrespectfully. He constantly corrects them."

"The teachers are intimidated by him, that's all. He only speaks out when they're wrong. They should be grateful. I mean, you don't listen to someone who has bad breath and just act like everything's okay, do you? You tell them."

"I will take your thoughts into consideration."

His demeanor was beginning to irritate me. I could tell he considered himself on a plane of intelligence beyond our comprehension.

"So, what's wrong with him?"

"That's why I'm here, ma'am."

"Oh, there's something in him," a voice cut through the room.

The sponge had finally lost some of his emotional girth.

"Explain," Dominic said curiously.

"I see it in his eyes." my father spoke, nodding his head, his thick, country accent causing him to lose credibility in the educated man's eyes.

"Go on."

"Sure, he don't say much. Reads all day, does his chores and the like, but it's when you watch him – when he thinks no one's lookin'. That's when you see the real him. You see his thoughts run and these ideas floating around that should never come to light. I got no proof, but I know my son. I know what he is."

The educated man was not impressed.

"Again, I am listening to every word you have to say, but at this time I think it would be most beneficial...for all of us, if I talk to Vincent alone."

"Do what you must," my father said with award-winning bravado - always the man's man. He swiped my mother's hand and led her away before she could say a word. Dominic kept up his façade until they were completely gone, locking the door the moment they shut it. He adjusted his glasses and sighed heavily, sticking his right hand in a pocket. He stood over me, letting every breath he took resonate with confidence. Subtly, he peeked at the one-way glass mirror, smiled, and parted his lips to speak.

The curtain rose.

"I assume from our exchange earlier that you abhor the thought of small talk or playing games, am I right?"

"I wouldn't say abhor," I said mockingly, "but you're right. I hate playing games, probably more than you do."

"Then let's skip the charades and get to the grit of it."

"Your move."

Dominic cleared his throat.

"When you were found, you were sitting by a tree reading a book, while an injured student – a result of your actions - was dying at your feet. Hardly normal. The teacher who reported you stated that even if you had not been the culprit, it would be rather strange to say you just stumbled upon him and decided to take out a book and enjoy the ambiance while he died beneath your feet. The examiner said he could have been bleeding anywhere from five to ten minutes. So, my question is, what were you doing there?"

"The real question should be: how is Donald considered a student?"

"I thought you hated playing games, Vincent," Dominic stated through pursed lips, temperate but firm.

"I hate when people play games with me. Playing with them is fine."

"You're not smart, Vincent."

"My record would defend me."

"Hardly. It convicts you."

"Okay, now you've got my attention."

"Vincent, I already have you figured out," he said, smiling like he knew some deep secret, "but I had to see how you would react to my initial question – to confirm my suspicions - and I'm pleased that you did not disappoint. I've only met one other person like you in my life. The odds of meeting two, so similar, were beyond my expectations."

"What are you talking about?"

"If you were like your classmate, the bully – I mean just like him...a depressing home life, horrible grades, lack of discipline, no motivation whatsoever – then I could understand what you did, as strange as that sounds. You'd be off the hook. I wouldn't even have come here to talk to you personally. God knows I could have saved on the gas."

"I'm sorry...did you just say that because I'm on the honor roll, I'm disciplined, and I have an adequate upbringing – my actions are worse? I'm the suspicious one? That makes no sense. Is our justice system really that off?"

"The justice system is fine. I'm here for preventive measures."

"Oh, okay, so what's next? I get sent to juvie? Is that what you mean by preventive measures? For beating up a criminal in self-defense and getting good grades? I hope minors get trial by jury because I'll just let you explain yourself and I'll walk free."

"Listen, Vincent, you're still a kid," he said matter-of-factly, "so let me dumb it down for you."

Again, that self-righteous, high-and-mighty tone adults loved to use. I had no qualm against adults displaying their knowledge and experience - it was how I learned. Through books, I experienced others' mistakes and how to capitalize on them. I became proficient in the art of conversation by reading dialogue. By observing my mother, I learned how to glide through social gatherings and dinner parties with the grace of a swan. From my father, I noticed that it wasn't who you were, but how you were perceived. The aptly named sponge was deemed a rock in many of high society's circles.

The bottom line was that I could not be anyone without their contribution and expertise; however, at no time should they underestimate my ability to adapt based on numerical age. I valued one's experiences and opinions, but age was not the basis for their worth. I would be more inclined to ask for educational advice from a recent high school valedictorian than a forty-year-old high school dropout. I've seen child therapists become abusive parents as their wild seed turned into early mothers and deadbeat fathers. People that acted like they knew the secrets of the universe but couldn't make ends meet. Starving dreamers and hypocritical Christians, religious murderers and suicidal motivational speakers. Only people who actually produced the results they lectured to others were worth listening to. Regrettably for Dominic, he wasn't following this same principle. He was simply calculating my worth on the barbaric, uncivilized concept of age.

"Explain it to me," I snapped back at him, ready to counter anything he had to say.

"Vincent, the fact of the matter is that you have the behavior and profile of a criminal intellect. You see, that high school dropout, the gang members, the drug dealers, they're of no concern to me. Sure, they're not completely stupid. They have their own mind and great pride in their street intelligence – able to elude capture and devise countless ways to achieve their immoral goals - but they will never know how the world works. Never. They've been so entangled in their own world for so long they are blind to everything else. All they can see is their own personal insignificant world and they get angry when no one will conform to it. They can't see that it's simply impossible for an entire population to comply in such a manner. So, they lie to themselves and go through life believing they are a master of all when they are really fools that accomplish nothing of substance. They always get caught in the end. They think it's normal to do jail time or go on welfare. Because they have a nice car and a new pair of Jordans, they are stuck in the illusion that they have accomplished something, when no one praises them but the few friends they have amassed. That type of man, that foolish, prideful and confused man, is a small matter. He will make no impact on the world unless it is of negative value, and even then, his actions will be no more unique than those of the other thugs around him, but you – you are different. You have the potential to be far more damaging to our society."

Dominic did not stop to let me reply.

"An idiot like the one fore-mentioned would've reveled in victory over his fallen foe. The average man would be terrified of his deed: broken, in shock over the control he lost, or paranoid that some hand of justice will inevitably bring down the hammer. But strangely enough, you were neither, and by remaining neutral, you made a choice. Maintaining a poker face condemned you. You were calm, and too cold to the mush lying at your feet – as if he didn't matter at all. Like he was an ant you had just crushed beneath your heel. Am I right?"

I couldn't respond. I had to hear more. Because of the way I acted, he had somehow managed to look past my flesh and peer into my very soul. He was describing me in ways I had never known even though I had met him only minutes ago. Who was this man?

"This is a crucial time, Vincent. Bringing you in was a priority because this is when you will surely begin to justify your act from within, and, ultimately, define yourself based upon it. You will try to believe that bringing that boy to your own version of justice felt good, and given the control over your emotions, you could do it again, with your criminal intellect helping you get away with it. I'm telling you right now that it's pointless. Not only will we be keeping a close eye on you, but you know deep down that any illegal act you perform will be wrong. If you choose a criminal lifestyle, you'll think that you're justified based on how people have treated you all your life. But then you would be no different than a thug, wouldn't you, Vincent? Justification – isn't that what they do? Isn't that what they do, Vincent?"

"Yeah...all of them," I said monotonously. His filibuster had taken all the fight out of me. He had done this before.

"Don't succumb to those thoughts. There's no benefit in it. No reward. Do you understand me?"

Silence.

"Can I ask you a question?" I asked innocently.

"Of course. Anything."

"You're not a psychologist, are you? You said that for my parents' sake."

"I'm not a psychologist," he confirmed. "I'm a criminal intelligence analyst. I specialize in handling people of your profile."

"And do you have a criminal intellect?"

"I do, Vincent, and that is why I can read the signs. Why I figured you out from the start."

"You use your criminal intellect to catch other potential criminals?"

"That's right."

"Okay," I nodded in defeat, "that's all I want to know."

"So, have I made myself crystal clear?"

"Crystal."

"I won't see you again face to face?"

"No, sir."

"No more trouble?"

"No," I replied flatly.

"Good. Then you're free to go. I'll be surveilling you from a distance. Remember, you're better than this. Don't become one of them."

I nodded to his satisfaction and like a wounded animal, practically limped out of the door to my expectant parents. Dominic watched me the entire time, taking in my body language, the little ticks I was unaware of, the way I approached my guardians. My mother hugged me and my father reluctantly rubbed my shoulders, but I wasn't aware of their condolences. All I could think of was the criminal intelligence analyst standing in the doorway, solving the Rubik's Cube that was me. I couldn't help but wonder if I passed the test, if my body language betrayed my thoughts to him unawares. The question lingered in my mind even as my parents led me out the door with heavy hearts: Did Dominic believe me? I wouldn't have, and if his intellect was half of what he claimed, he didn't either.

He was right on all accounts. I was better than them. They moved like animals, no rhyme or reason to their actions but simple primitive instinct. I was not so lucky. My love of simplicity and ignorance could no longer comply with what now consumed my thoughts. It was no longer an appreciation for Jason's compassion. It was no longer a drive to naively create a world void of pain and suffering. This new revelation was something I could envelop completely...

Dominic had unintentionally showed me the path.

My criminal intellect, or C.I.

The phrase sounded like an ice cube sliding down my tongue during a blazing hot summer barbecue. The appeal sent chills down my spine as I took hold of destiny. Dominic, in all his grandeur, had made one terrible mistake. At the time of our meeting, I had hated being treated poorly because of my age, but that did not mean I was at full maturity. You see, he had made the mistake of labeling me, and the label he gave me was too big to simply ignore.

I was not a stranger to labeling. Whether it's a passing insult from a classmate or a teacher making sure you knew you were retarded, labels were a daily occurrence. However, it is up to the individual how much weight each label carries, and none had stuck to me so far.

But now I had willingly received and accepted my label. A goal and a principle to abide by, for Dominic, this man who had rendered me speechless through an analysis of my classmates, intrigued me. He explained my peers in a clairvoyant way that I had already discovered myself, but had been unable to express articulately. The epiphany that we shared a similar thought pattern was equally thrilling, but...I would not pursue his career.

He was smart, but there was so much more he could do. Why spend his intelligence on those whose fate you've figured out a long time ago? No. That was a life well-wasted. Calling one a bully, no matter how articulate and grandiose you made it sound, was still calling one a bully. So, my course would be quite different from his. I decided to use my criminal intellect for my own ambitions. The possibilities were endless. And just like Dominic had said, I could use my C.I. to make sure I got away with everything, saving my jail cell for my peers...

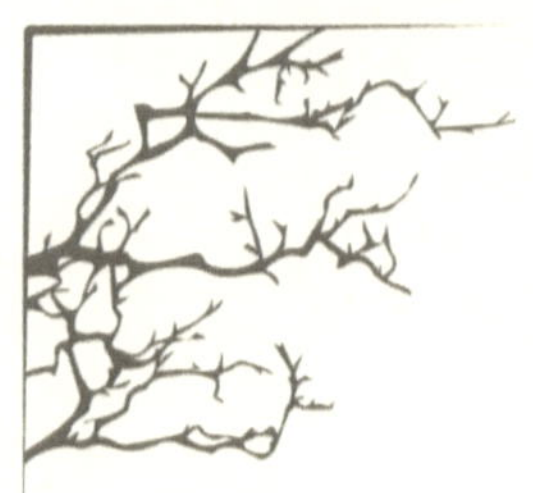

CHAPTER 3:
TRAINING

I believed Dominic when he said that he would be "surveilling me from a distance" so I knew that I couldn't jump right into full use of my C.I; I had to be patient. At school I masqueraded as an ambitious student with a fear of all authority, not much of a change from how I used to be, while my true self remained in hibernation, coming out only for a season to feed so that it would not die. I was sure I didn't know from what angle Dominic was watching, so during my years of solitude, very much like an inmate in a penitentiary, I would train on my own with little distraction but I wasn't training my muscles, but my mind. I arbitrarily stood on the sidelines, watching as the world passed by.

My parents reacted normally, my run-in with the law being a minor blip in my life. My father's claim that he saw some kind of evil within me seemed to have been forgotten for he went back to his buffet of Doritos and primetime television immediately. He had only made comments about me to impress Dominic, nothing more. Mother went back to her two jobs and let stress overtake any worry she had of me. Teachers, classmates – they all treated me the same. No one knew about my talk with Dominic or how I was labeled as having a criminal intellect. In fact, because Donald had beaten up quite a bit before I lashed out, everyone just assumed I went to the hospital, that Donald's brush with death wasn't a result of the wrath of Vincent, but a gang member or a mysterious mugger. At times, I was very entertained by the stories people came up with. But not Jason.

I told him the story of how I fought back, how I was found by administration and taken in for questioning at the police station. Once I relayed my side of the incident, they let me go. I couldn't tell him about the meeting. I wanted to, but Jason was just so noble, I didn't want to taint his image of me. His childish sense of honor and the greater good reminded me of a time in which I too believed in such things, and through Jason, I could still glimpse them once in a while, and hope for a moment. But one thing had to remain certain. My friend, my only real friend must not see the monster within me, for even creatures needed someone to talk to, if only superficially.

I was sure he saw some kind of change in me. How could he not? I once bathed in light as he did, but now the light blinded me to the point I could no longer see. Darkness was more appealing now, and even with all of my carefully chosen words and cover-ups, he could see the light within me fading. He never brought it up, but I saw it in his raised eyebrows, or how he would quickly change a conversation. We were the best of friends that knew nothing about each other. And I needed that.

I could draw no more attention to myself if my plans were to work. My body moved autonomously – school, girlfriends, petty crime – basically a normal teenage existence, putting my hand into the mix only after excessive planning and foolproof execution:

SEVENTEEN YEARS OLD

November 5th

An acquaintance decides to dump a tray of mushy cafeteria food on my head after I tell him what his future will be if he doesn't stop insulting a friend of mine. I play the victim, inflicting wounds onto my body for presentation, crying to the principal with forced tears, threatening parental involvement and media belligerence if he doesn't take action against a student that should've been expelled years ago. Jason watches in horror as I pay others to come forward with similar stories, former victims with a thirst for vengeance. Pressure rises and the super senior graduates with no diploma in hand.

December 15th

My family makes our annual trip to my relatives' lodge in New Hampshire. I'm eventually confided in by my aunt who reveals what my spoiled cousin's Christmas gift is going to be this year – a brand new iPhone. I already have a plan formulated.

I make a deal with my spoiled cousin, Oliver. I plant the idea in his head that his mom got him socks for Christmas. When he asks why, I tell him it's because of all the holes in his current ones (caused by yours truly). I wait ten minutes to let the idea marinate then I boost his ego. I whine how he still gets the best gifts and I'll give him ten bucks for any one of them. He agrees and says only if he gets to choose which one. Of course, I say. They are his gifts, after all.

December 24th

Oliver inspects the sizes of all the elegantly wrapped gifts under the tree and chooses the smallest one – the one that must be you-know-what. He gives it to me humbly and greedily takes my ten dollars. He asks when I'll open it, and I say later, when I can show all my friends what a great gift is in there. He giggles and I feign stupidity.

December 25th

Oliver opens his gifts with the fury of a hurricane, becoming more torrential as he finds no socks amongst them. The best gift he gets is a steel thermos that keeps liquids hot or cold. I see my aunt look confused so I pull her aside and tell her that Oliver had taken the iPhone last night. I had told him accidentally despite my vow of secrecy (oh, how I apologized). Somehow, it just slipped out. I tell her it's best to confront him tomorrow about taking gifts early because no one wants to be grounded on Christmas. Besides, think how embarrassing it would be for her if she was scolding her child on the Lord's Birthday! She forgets my age and follows my words.

December 26th

My family leaves ritualistically early. Oliver will learn what happened, but by then I'll be home. Next time I'll say I'm too old for trivial family gatherings.

EIGHTEEN YEARS OLD

January 18th

My mother hands me a newspaper obituary. Apparently, Dominic had met an untimely death at the hands of one of his former clients. It's impossible that I had any involvement in the matter based on the time and location, but my father claims that he will now be Dominic's eyes.

Hilarious.

February 16th

With careful observation and study, I come to the conclusion that no one has taken on Dominic's case concerning me. Though I realize I may still be looked at periodically, there is no real cause for worry. Now that he is gone, I doubt there are many people left in the world with the capability to stop me once I put my full potential into a plan. I ponder what I should do with my life after I graduate from high school. My old childhood idea of Eclosion begins to sound appealing.

February 20th

I concentrate my efforts on the increasingly popular Jason Reynolds. Our friendship has become more strained since my "awakening" but I keep him on a short leash by setting up scenarios in which others betray him with gossip, lies and uncovered secrets. This makes the world around him become his enemy while I remain his sole friend. He also needs me now more than ever – true to the football stereotype, his grades begin to slack and he wants to continue being quarterback of the football team. I promise to help him make general honors (because that's what friends do – help one another). The perfectly dumb athlete loses any suspicions of my change in recent behavior, and we begin to establish a solid friendship, just like old times...

March 8th

I notice my father still looks at me with suspicion, even with my recent angelic behavior. This is not good, especially considering that I have decided upon an endgame for my life. I want to start a company, probably in health and life insurance due to its constant growth, but my company will have a hidden agenda. An agenda that will carry out my true desires. If this sounds familiar at all, it should, for it is exactly the Eclosion model I came up with Jason years ago. Except now, I can take it to a more global level. However, if I'm to even come close to making this a reality, I need to rouse no suspicion, even if it's from my father. I will need to deal with him somehow. So, understanding that those with an excellent reputation can get away with much, I formulate a plan.

March 12th

I purchase a small notebook and begin to religiously observe my father's behavior and habits, looking for flaws in his character that I can exploit. Everyone has them. Better to have him convict himself than make something up.

April 28th

After keeping an accurate log of his routines, I thoroughly inspect it, not only for habitual behaviors, but also for any inconsistencies that could alter my plan. I'm satisfied with the results. Adults are creatures of conformity and ritual, and I notice that he spends a great deal of time drinking coffee. When he consumes it, he can be awake for long periods of time, but without it, he crashes almost instantly, especially with food as a catalyst. His slumber is even stronger than usual then. I can use that.

April 29th

I decide to take his coffee to school – all of it. Before he can wake up, I stuff the large Folger's can into my backpack, knowing that I'll have to come up with excuses of why I couldn't fit my textbooks in later. If I'm found with the coffee before I can get rid of it, I'll make the excuse that I was planning on selling it for profit. It makes a lot of sense considering so many of my classmates are obsessed with energy drinks –

eating raw coffee grounds wasn't unfathomable in the mind of a teacher. It's a Monday so my mother will be busy at work all day and most of the night. My father, who is habitually unemployed, will be lazily watching television into the late hours of the night. All I have to do, at this point, is throw out the coffee.

I dump the coffee ground into a trash can that's often filled quickly and changed like clockwork. I fill the empty coffee can with dirt and plant some uncommon flowers into it before I place it on my chemistry teacher's desk. With all the hard work she's putting into educating us, she deserves a gift or two now and then.

I bring Jason with me in between classes, making sure to lead him with conversation as we walk the crowded hallways. We talk about simple subjects at first – movies, videogames – until we walk by an area infested with the Lost, my name for those whom Dominic had said were of no concern in life. I stop, as if I can't walk at the same time, leaning up against a wall that was within earshot of their group. I sigh, annoyed, saying how I'm sick of leaving my back door unlocked because my mom never remembers to bring her house keys to work and we sleep like rocks so no one would hear her cries if she was locked out. I vaguely sense the Lost taking notes, and Jason, on cue, asks if she could just stay with a neighbor. We have had this conversation before, so it doesn't seem out of the ordinary to discuss, and besides, Jason always asks the right questions at the right time. I say how my neighbor is never home, as if 136 Plainville Road was the plague, adding that he was probably out gambling his earnings away, which he usually complained about to anyone who would listen.

I figure it is enough information for the time being. If my plan doesn't come to fruition, new tactics will be employed. I bank on the fact that the Lost aren't patient when it comes to instant gratification, so I will be expecting them tonight. I only hope they aren't dumb enough to get the wrong house.

I keep walking after the knowledge is intentionally exchanged, and my loyal puppy follows obediently.

April 29th – afternoon

I read my father as much as possible for any changes in his personal schedule, but all is normal. He's had a long day searching for jobs so he's ready to lounge. I count on predictability and make him a huge dinner, cooking slow to waste time, the evening creeping ever so slowly upon him. He eats greedily and in bulk, finishes, sighs, and lets lethargy wash the food down. I already know what will happen next. He asks for coffee, to help him fight through his drowsiness, and I inform him that there isn't any left. Before he gets alarmed, I explain that Mom is gone for the night working overtime and I have homework to do. He says he needs it but I tell him respectfully that Mark's is closed already (making sure to mention the only grocery store that was closed at that hour). My father decides to wrestle fate once more before he goes belly up into slumber.

April 29th – evening/night

My father is asleep now, in his favorite recliner in the middle of the living room. I make sure the back door is unlocked. Hopefully, they have the brains to skip the front. My father is snoring like a dragon now, his stomach protruding slightly larger than before. I have my preparations ready at this point, but my expected visitors don't arrive until 1 a.m. My mother is still burning the midnight oil, and for her sake, it is well that she does so. Even I barely hear them break in, and I was waiting for them diligently. They are professionals at their craft, stealthy and experienced, already comparing values of the merchandise they see on the shelves. I wait until they inevitably see the safe in the office, suspiciously wide open, with the picture that covers it removed and placed to the side. They don't have the fortitude to question why it's open; greed consumes their caution. I hear them mumbling down below as I strain my ears upstairs, above the office. Excited whispers gain volume. I don't miss my cue as I shove a chair down the stairs, a game I invented three months prior to test the limits of my father's slumber. The few occasions I had been caught by my mother, (never my father) I had said I was trying to sneak out of the house to go to a friend's place or a party – typical teenage alibis.

Apparently, my father hasn't hit the REM cycle. The chair tumbling down the stairs wakes my father and startles the intruders. He moves immediately, instinctively, heading to the stairs as fast as manageable to catch me, but he stops when he hears movement in the office, the room with no windows, no exits. He moves cautiously, and two of the Lost jump him. I can't see the shuffle, but based on their brutality and my father's grunts, they have the upper hand. I had counted on their animalistic fury, for all animals claw and bite their way out of trouble when they're cornered. Soon the blows halt the breathing and I make my move, running back to my room, calling out their names like I was taking attendance in school, letting the intruders know that I couldn't be allowed to escape.

I run across the hall hard in stride, emphasizing each step. They barrel up the stairs, practically clamoring over each other for my life. They slam open my bedroom door with authority, and I answer with mine. Without hesitation, I fire the entire clip of my father's .45 Long Colt revolver, steadying my breath for accuracy, remembering to adjust the angle to compensate for the kick. They fall as my bullets fall with them: lifeless and full of residue. They thud softly, their jackets breaking their irrevocable fall. The giants groan and writhe but I silence them quickly as I load six more rounds into them, just in case. I drop the gun to the floor afterwards, and wait. I do not know the fate of my father, but it makes no sense to inspect him, in case he survived the attack and I would be obligated to help him. No, it was better to remain upstairs.

April 30th – Early morning

The police come, and strangely I half-expect Dominic to show up, even though that's impossible. Shots in my house had been heard and called in by the neighbors. Once again, I play the humanity card without shame – tears, shaking, stuttering over the two men I killed. I tell the police that when I had heard the intruders break in and attack my father, I had retrieved the gun and loaded it. Though I should've, I had not gone downstairs; I was way too scared.

Apparently, I had done the right thing for my ulterior motive by staying put – my father had been beaten without mercy but had remained awake after I killed the two intruders. According to the coroner, he could have been saved, but without immediate assistance, he had died of blood loss before the paramedics arrived.

Mom is dealing with it.

May 5th

Funeral was nice.

May 8th

I wake up from a nightmare in a cold sweat. I don't feel guilty for what I've done, but my subconscious must. From this day on, I spend more time training my heart and mind to feel less. Jason, the only one capable of possibly sensing a change within me, doesn't notice anything. He's too busy with sports to think much anymore. All he talks about is how lucky I am to survive the ordeal, and why, out of all people, would they choose my house to rob.

June 13th

I decide to leave home. My mother is devastated, but understands. My reason is that I "haven't been the same" since Dad died. How true that is.

NINETEEN YEARS OLD

January 28th

With my father's life insurance and the support of my mother's small investments, I begin my endgame – the last plan I will ever need to carry out, though it will be a long journey. I start out by founding a small upstart health insurance corporation called...you guessed it, Eclosion. It is simply an insurance agency. I give out ridiculously low rates on my policies to attract people in the beginning, and wait for my clientele to grow before I start discussing my true motives with a selected few. Many are excited to hear my real plans, and the low premiums don't hurt either since I'm not in it to make billions of dollars. Jason Reynolds becomes my equal partner in the company and talks excitedly everyday about changing the world. He finally gets what Eclosion is supposed to be about.

May 3rd

I appoint Jason Reynolds as the figurehead and public face of Eclosion. I decide to stay in the background, secretly making all of the major decisions. Jason is happy to be the leader of anything and I am content with the choice – he is popular, handsome and very sociable – many things that one could argue I wasn't. With Jason as the public face of the company, Eclosion is an easy sell as the next up-and-coming insurance agency.

May 20th

With the company making small profits, I begin my true purpose: to infiltrate every major aspect of society. I place our recruit members and clients within the governmental, medical, financial, security, and even education sectors of the nation. The plan is to have many of my employees secretly work for Eclosion part-time while they stay in their original places of employment full-time. They will rise through the ranks until they are the bosses and then I will give them orders on how to rule. I have this plan so that eventually Eclosion will secretly rule most of the country and be able to carry out decisions which will help it run more efficiently. Jason has been waiting for this moment for years and does his job as the leader beautifully. His charisma is unparalleled and all who hear his voice follow his commands. Though I still hold all the power in my hands, I can't help but become a little jealous – if I decided to publicly become the CEO, would the masses accept me over him?

September 26th

With Jason as the face of Eclosion, people are joining at a rapid rate. We approach specific people and explain why we need their services. No one turns us down. The economy is too bad and the government is practically non-existent. We need hope, and Eclosion is the answer. Most of the people we choose already have high positions in their places of employment, so they are able to rapidly make some much-needed changes. We are very particular about who we hire, though we aren't exclusive. Even entry level employees get the opportunity to work part time for our insurance sector, and full time for our hidden agenda. Nevertheless, all must adhere to one rule: that no one is to speak about what Eclosion does secretly. No one.

TWENTY YEARS OLD

January 27th

Eclosion has grown exponentially and Jason is loved by many; however, like anything else that involves groups of people, there is disagreement amongst our members. In order to make sure unity holds together, I decide to play the dissension in the ranks. I do this for two reasons: one, so I can reign in those that are disgruntled in the company and give them a voice, and two, I can cast any suspicion of me being the real leader behind the scenes and put the spotlight solely on Jason. My new followers, the dissenters, cry that Jason is too soft and cautious, so I say that I am a man of action. They say they want me take over the leadership of Eclosion, and even raise funds to donate to this cause. I don't intend to take the throne just yet, so I pocket the money I receive for my own private use. This plan of "divide and conquer" is working better than I imagined. The model, which I stole from my nation's republican and democratic parties, works beautifully, for now Jason and I can continue our goals while it seems like the people actually have a voice. All of the fence jumpers and undecided follow my lead, while the rest are sheep, led by the shepherd that is my puppet. Ultimately, I am in control of everyone within the corporation.

March 8th

As numbers have exceeded into the hundreds of thousands, Jason and I establish a board of directors who will vote for policies we believe in. The purpose is to make the people believe that they get to decide who represents them, when they really don't. During this process I also decide to pursue more domesticated endeavors by marrying a young woman in the organization. Since I will soon have Jason appoint me as heir to the throne (and therefore I will become the next CEO of Eclosion), I will need the people to support me as much as possible, which they are more likely to do if you have a family. It shows you have a heart.

TWENTY ONE YEARS OLD

September 23rd

Jason is beginning to win over my "dissenters" group in the company. Doesn't he remember that division is part of the plan? Doesn't he remember that I am in control of that half? For some reason, his speeches have included more improvisation lately. He's not sticking to the scripts I give him. What's this all about? Where is this coming from? He's a busy man but we must talk.

October 5th

After a heated discussion, Jason vows to never overstep his boundaries again, and that from now on he will stick to the script. I don't believe him, but it will have to do for now. Amidst my victory, my daughter, Katherine, is born.

TWENTY TWO YEARS OLD

April 2nd

Jason, my marionette, appoints an heir to Eclosion's public and private sector. And it's not me. Somehow he even gets the board of directors to back this decision. The heir he now appointed will inherit all responsibilities, exclusive rights, and benefits as chief executive officer, in the event of Jason's death. This new prince, Ivan, is brash and short-tempered, with a bloodlust only a piranha would be proud of. I don't know why Jason chose him, or what his qualifications could possibly be since he's only joined Eclosion a short time ago, but I do know one thing - my puppet is becoming a real boy, getting too comfortable in his position. He's obviously forgotten who created him. The only reason Jason could've possibly chosen Ivan without my consent is that he's about to make a move against me. Should Jason mysteriously die, I would now have Ivan to contend with. A man that knows nothing of my control over Eclosion.

May 2nd

Jason Reynolds is gunned down in a drive-by shooting while going for a walk in the suburbs, a mile from his house. Someone must have known his schedule. Good thing he appointed an heir.

May 6th

Ivan is officially ordained as the CEO of Eclosion. With no "official" power within the company, there was no way I could overturn the inauguration.

May 8th

Ivan takes over Jason's assets. Jason's memorabilia is boxed and placed in a shrine for him to be remembered. The items are deemed sacred and my Pinocchio is revered as a saint. All I want to do is cry.

May 10th

Though I have laid low since Jason's death, I am confronted by Ivan who demands my loyalty and support. He remembers I cried out against many of Jason's policies in public. I pretend I'm scared and swear my allegiance, vowing to stay out of his way and keep my opinions to myself. My influence is greatly diminished and fades within a few days. I am nothing more than a ghost now.

June 12th (later to be remembered as the "Mourning Massacre")

Ivan wastes little time in displaying his authority, having many government officials murdered early this morning by some of our employees – operatives tasked to carry out the hard decisions. It's a stupid plan because Ivan doesn't realize that murder doesn't outright solve the problem. The officials he killed will just be replaced by those of similar stature. At the very least he could have set it up so some of our people would fill in the positions, but he didn't even do that. Still, the massacre goes off without a clue of who coordinated it. After all, who would expect a physical therapist to just suddenly start killing people? Or a doctor? Or an ice cream truck man? The attacks are swift and carried out only on this day, ensuring that the whole world knows that it was not a coincidence. Gang members, under a false promise of joining our secret club, commit most of the heinous acts and are left in the dust afterwards. The gangs aren't happy, especially when many of their members are apprehended, but Ivan, who has promised that Eclosion will no longer be an organization of inaction, is ecstatic.

August 15th

It is now one month after the "Mourning Massacre." The FBI, who have been putting together the pieces of the puzzle, release a press release stating they believe there is a secret organization behind the murders, and that anyone with information on its structure or members should contact them immediately. Fortunately, our employees are too disgruntled with how the country is run to provide information. Still, Ivan is surely not the type to start planning his actions out now. In his spontaneity, he will make mistakes - it's in his nature to do so.

December 22nd

I am not a superstitious man, but for the second time in my life, I wake up in a cold sweat after a string of nightmares. I sense a storm is coming...

CHAPTER 4:
SERENITY [Day 0/
8]{Dec 24th – 10 A.M}

"**C**an you move over? You smell like mold."

"You look like mold," I muttered, ready for the hurricane.

My wife battered me with velvet blows as I buried my head into the pillow. I pretended to snore as she kicked my leg. I snored louder.

"When was the last time you showered?"

"The last time I needed to." I sighed as she jumped out of bed, threw the comforter on the floor, and recklessly ran down the stairs. She'd be back, and with a vengeance.

I turned over and stared aimlessly through the skylight above me. The sun was directly on my face and it spotlighted the room. What a Christmas Eve this was. At least if it had been snowing, the death-like gray would have matched my mood, but instead the star of our galaxy mocked me with blinding laughs as it pierced my eyes. I turned away in annoyance clutching my goose down pillow for comfort, but even the pillow seemed illuminated in the golden rays. I should've kept my eyes shut and ignored my wife's complaining, but for the hundredth time I thought that if I acknowledged her, she would stop talking. Nope. Now I had to deal with the fact that I only had three hours of sleep because I had stayed up all night staring into space, wondering how to get my life together. And I couldn't go back to sleep, because she was sure to prance up the stairs any moment to deny me any comfort. There was no point to anything anymore. I used to have it so good. Everything had been planned out until Jason just had to make a move against me. Now

I was just a regular 9-to-5 guy attempting to stay out of Ivan's radar...did the sun just get brighter?

I gave the skylight a wary eye, silently loathing its existence over my bed as the sun increased its brilliance, mocking me.

Oh, and what a reason to mock me it had, for today I would be spending the day with my family - a family that I started. You would think that as the head of the household I would possess all of the voting power, but I soon discovered that being a husband and a father was nothing like running a company. It took work, and the kind I was unaccustomed to...the emotional kind. Sure, I knew going into marriage that a husband died daily, I just didn't know how many times. Each day was taxing on my mental capacity.

Like adopting a kid, my wife came with her own baggage to sort through, including years of social experience that she thought I somehow enjoyed. I would smile and laugh at the jokes she got from the internet, and chuckle as small talk evolved into internal suicide, but despite these moments, I had to admit, there were times when it wasn't all bad.

In the beginning...it wasn't bad at all. Back then, I could have settled the moment I decided that I needed a wife, but like Jason, I made sure I chose wisely. My courtship of Isabel Castillo did not start out a romantic one - a typical oscillation of chocolates and roses, gifts on anniversaries, hours of dancing and sweet talks. It was a grand matter of circumstance and mutual understanding. Even I was in awe of her beauty, and how she possessed the grace of a professional ballet dancer. She could captivate with majesty and elegance that caused great envy amongst her same-gendered peers. Yet even then, this was not what held my interest. It was her passion.

To many she was passive and tame, but at the optimal moment she would unleash her fury like a lion devouring its prey, taking either her career or her social status to new heights. She knew how to play the game as well as I did, and I admired her tenacity to hold on to her beliefs in the face of danger and come out victorious. A risk-taker, I was not, but

I knew that with a partner who was, I could learn the art - for when I would become king of this world, I would need all the delicacy of a hammer. Only she, a logical yet passionate creature, could teach this proud being what he lacked, so, I made it my business to make her my wife.

Within a few minutes of meeting of her, I had told her, "I'm going to marry you someday, and you are going to be the happiest woman on Earth."

She believed me, and she should have. She knew when a man spoke what he was worth. She saw the reality of things, and this I loved. I could have chosen a woman of the romantic comedy type, situated within an abundance of giggly female friends whose lives orbited their respective men, but I wanted someone who knew that love was more than just emotion, that it was about mutual companionship, respect and understanding. These things were far more concrete than feelings. If I wanted a slobbering airhead that begged to be petted and held all the time, I'd have bought a dog.

Instead of settling for less, I now had a partner to share in my forbidden dance of the immoral. I shared my secrets candidly, and she kept them well. I only hid one thing from her: that I was the secret founder and leader of Eclosion. I wanted to tell her, but I couldn't risk someone finding out. No matter how close she got to me, that was one secret that will forever divide us; nevertheless, I had to admit, whenever she talked of how great of a leader Jason was, I was tempted...

My thoughts were interrupted as a tidal wave of cold water smashed into my face. I heard my wife giggle, scampering down the stairs, a plastic bucket echoed mockingly on the wooden floor. I spurted some stray water out of my mouth and shuffled off of the bed awkwardly, planning her demise before hastily pursuing. I loved this game and though I never admitted it, she knew. Sometimes I wouldn't even see it coming - Isabel's booby traps in the house - miscellaneous pieces of ice on the kitchen floor or Tabasco hot sauce in the coffee - keeping my mind sharp in times of peace and boredom. She was a perfect proctor that was incapable of crossing the line, for even in her success, she was no more in control than a student to his master. No matter how many times a student desires to become the authority, the fact remains that the master can choose at any time to put the student down. Camaraderie was good, but it didn't change the fact that I needed her on a short leash. Who better to serve such a purpose than a woman?

The weight of my wet clothes, sticking to me like a second skin, brought my thoughts closer to home. Going to bed fully dressed was an annoying habit of mine that I wasn't planning on breaking any time soon - a precaution, in case I had to make a clean getaway in the middle of the night. My wife refused to join in my little idiosyncrasies, claiming that sometimes I was a little too paranoid for her tastes. Did she even remember who we worked for?

The thought of her judgments stoked the fire beneath me and suddenly I was ready for the hunt. I crept out of the bedroom, anticipating an assault, when a stumbling block was cast in my way - my daughter. A little more than a year old, she was noticeably a shadow of her father - she didn't say much, but her subtlety, choice of words, and body language revealed all.

"Dada?" she mumbled, pulling up on the pajamas that were too big for her, her auburn hair curled in her mother's signature fashion.

"What is it, Katie?"

I didn't particularly like the name Katie or Katherine, but her mother was persistent about the matter.

Katie inquisitively pointed to my clothes. I chuckled as I interpreted her question. I bent down on one knee to look her in the eye. Out of the corner of my eye, I vaguely noticed the tan carpet hadn't been vacuumed in weeks as a quarter sized tumbleweed of hair blew past us. Katie put half of her right thumb in her mouth and began to fidget side-to-side - a tick that somehow enhanced her ability to listen. I placed a hand on her shoulder as I told her the harsh truth.

"It was Mommy," I replied solemnly, bowing my head in defeat. She nodded in agreement, for she had known the answer from the beginning.

"Don't worry though," I said cheerfully. "I'll get her back."

She smiled to this and I saw that she was pleased with my response, though she still refused to accompany me downstairs on my back. I had once told her that it was called a piggyback ride, but when she had discovered what a pig actually was (courtesy of her favorite children's book), she had suddenly loathed the concept, for I looked nothing like a pig, making the term "piggyback ride" inaccurate and downright disrespectful. My wife claimed that there was no way Katie could have made such an analysis, but I recognized Katie's inner intelligence.

Katie passed up on the show that was about to commence and scurried back to her room where all the toys were. I immediately took flight down the stairs, skipping over the fifth and eighth stairs that creaked like a dying bird. So much time had been wasted already. Who knew what horrors Isabel had cooked up in that time?

I was dismayed to learn that there were no traps to spot and disassemble as I made my way to the bottom of the stairs, past the living room where I looked behind each couch and loveseat, and finally to the kitchen. Isabel stood in the middle of the room by the stove, talking on the phone with a grimaced look on her face. What a disappointment. The living room was usually the most exciting section to get through, for unlike the stairs, there were no creaking boards or chances of falling. The teal carpet lusciously provided a sound-proof walkway that made my approach unforeseeable. Isabel would usually compensate by having invisible trip wire in place, or she would be hiding somewhere ready to jump out and scare me. There were surprisingly many places to hide - behind the couch, in-between the dressers, or next to the curio cabinet. Despite the disgustingly bright carpet, the rest of the room had a mysteriously dark overcast that cast a variety of shadows around the furniture.

Isabel sighed irritably as she shifted her weight onto her right foot, the ivory-only colored phone barely cradled in her hand. Her voice was strained, so it could only be a handful of people on the other end of the phone. I began listing all the possibilities based on her rigid stance and lip-biting, her eyes full of disappointment. I held back a grin as I finally came to a conclusion. She turned to me immediately, with a hurt look in her eyes, as I spoke her concerns into existence.

"Ivan?" I asked, though I knew the answer. By asking questions, I constantly played the "average man." If I always let people know what I thought, what I interpreted and discovered, they would expect it from me. The concept was no different than the "smart kid" of the classroom that raised his hand at all times, portraying his vast knowledge of the subject material. Yes, he revealed his superiority, but he also received his reward. He would never be labeled as anything other than the "smart kid." I, on the other hand, was free to change my persona as the situation arose, a chameleon that's able to blend in with all backgrounds. Withholding the depth of my knowledge was one of my greatest and most effective weapons. For my opponents, ignorance indeed was bliss, until the moment I struck back.

"Yeah, it's Ivan," she sighed, chucking the phone down onto the kitchen counter. She pulled up on her nightgown strap, which had begun to fall from her shoulder, and blew up at some of her disarrayed hair. Preliminary tears readied to break through the dam in her eyes, but I had already begun to reach forward and cup her cheek in my palm, my left hand playing with her bed hair. Immediately she calmed down and smiled warmly into my eyes. I knew women were most susceptible to touch, thus heightening the effect of my words.

"He needs me at the office, doesn't he?"

"Yeah, but I really don't want you to go."

"I'll be back," I lamented gently, careful to maintain a façade of care.

"It's Christmas Eve. We're supposed to be spending time with my parents today."

"You know I'd be there if I could."

"Oh, you would now? You've been trying to get out of this for a month," she said, turning to put on water for coffee. Her feisty mood was coming out. She couldn't be all that disappointed.

"You have to admit I make a good point. Why shouldn't we skip your parents this year? Ever since Katie was born, we've barely had any time together, and Christmas is really the only vacation time we have. Eclosion rests for no one."

"You can't get out of it now, Vincent. You're going to my parents today, even if Ivan called you in."

"What do you want me to do? Call out? Tell Ivan I got sick all of a sudden?"

"No, I understand you have to go. Boss's orders - but, how long will you be gone?"

"Not sure, it depends. What did Ivan want?"

"He didn't say. He never does, and it's really annoying."

"He's just looking out for himself."

"What kind of leader only looks out for himself?" Her voice was beginning to crack.

"I'm surprised you're asking that. What kind of leader doesn't? He carries a huge burden on his shoulders. I bet there are times he wishes he could be one of the regular employees again."

"Yeah, but he could understand how I feel once in a while. It's the holidays, and he doesn't care one bit that he's taking you away from the family."

"He has to be reserved with you. For all he knows the phones could be tapped. He does have reason to be paranoid."

Better to play the loyal servant - give Ivan all the honor I could muster without throwing up.

"The phones are tapped?!"

"No-no. The phones could be."

"Ivan has been a fool since his inception," she said angrily. "He doesn't know what he's doing. When Jason was in office, he just treaded softly; there was no reason for him to tap phones and look over his shoulder because no one was chasing him."

"And look where that got him."

"So, you'd rather have these random tantrums Ivan throws out than Jason's careful planning? I know he died, but at least you have to admit it's not because of a mistake he made. Eclosion's enemies probably found out who he was and killed him."

"I think you should give Ivan a break. It's not an easy job being the CEO of such a powerful organization. Besides, ever since he took office, more people have joined our cause than ever before."

I didn't like talking about Jason at all, let alone his death.

"That's only because standards have dropped!" Isabel retorted. "Eclosion is becoming nothing more than a gang of thugs and walking statistics. If this continues - if he keeps on accepting all these random people - no one will remember us, Vincent. No one!"

"That's not what it's all about," I said solemnly. "That's never been what it's about."

"What do you mean?"

"Eclosion's purpose is to eliminate corruption and ensure that society goes the way we, as the people, want it to go. It's not about names or legacies. If we are remembered, then fine, but it will mean nothing if our accomplishments are only novelties. Our forefathers believed in a united nation, one free of hierarchy and sovereign rule, but no one remembers that. People just think it's nice to have time off on Veteran's Day."

"Well," she scoffed, "someone's heated about this."

Apparently, I had forgotten myself.

"Anyways," I cleared my throat, "if Ivan thinks that his ordinances will get us one step closer to our goal, we should support him. Jason chose him, and we should honor his wishes."

She raised an eyebrow as she darted a hand forward to feel my forehead.

"Are you feeling okay? Since when are you a Jason supporter?"

"Never," I grinned, "but we should honor his wishes...since he was our leader."

"You're right," she chuckled, seeing my uneasiness. "Ivan is the heir Jason wanted, though sometimes I wonder why."

"It's possible that Jason planned on taking a more aggressive role himself, choosing Ivan as a precaution, so that his plans were sure to go forward."

"You're just saying that to cheer me up," she smiled sweetly. "You hated Jason's policies. He's probably turning over in his grave right now hearing you say this."

Let's hope not.

"True...but I wouldn't have met you otherwise," I said slyly.

"Why's that?" she asked curiously, sure of the answer but needing to hear me say it.

"Because if you weren't such a Jason supporter, we'd never have caught each other's interest."

"Just fuel for the fire," she cooed as I saw that look in her eyes. This was getting dangerous.

"Speaking of fire, did Ivan say when I should be there?"

Her countenance fell, but by now she was calm, serene. It had been close. If I had allowed us to get intimate with each other, there was little chance I would have escaped her clutches later. Better to break it all off now.

"He said in about an hour. There's some meeting he wants you to attend," she said, refusing to look at my face directly.

"A meeting?"

Even I was confused.

"Yes," she confirmed, turning to scrounge around in the fridge.

"What for?"

"He doesn't tell me anything, remember?" she said in frustration, grabbing a carton of milk.

"Right...but I've never been to a formal meeting before, let alone with one of the executives."

"Nervous?"

"A little, actually. I wonder what this is all about."

Since I was feeling uneasy, and Isabel frequently complained that she desired to see more emotional reactions out of me, I figured it was better to allow this one.

"There's a first for everything, I guess - being nervous, secret executive meetings - just be home as soon as you can, okay?"

"Sure," I said, my thoughts already trailing off.

It was, of course, a lie that I had never been to a meeting - how could that be true considering I started the organization? I had made Jason carry a wire and a one-way receiver at all times. He would go to the meetings I called through him, regurgitating my dictations through his own words as I listened intensely. Although the new laws were actually mine, the board of directors credited them to Jason, and awed over his leadership. He played the role so beautifully; it was as if he had no strings to hold him down.

But since my foolish puppet had become a real boy, and started using his newly discovered brain, Ivan was now irrevocably in charge. I hadn't been able to eavesdrop at all. He ran a tight ship and his unpredictability was enough to scare me into dormancy - but like a volcano, I wouldn't stay dormant forever, and when I erupted, all in my path would be consumed by hellfire. If Ivan had called me to a meeting for the purpose I suspected, then my days were numbered, and I'd have to make a move very soon - any move to secure my future. He had known long ago that I was against his predecessor, and because of his tendency to hold grudges, it was only a matter of time before he had to fulfill his need to kill me. Called meeting or not, I had to tread very softly.

Since my awakening that fateful day in the schoolyard, I had never been defeated, especially once I had a plan in place. And a plan for Ivan I would have. I would craft his destruction, slow and elegant like a painter's brush – watching as the deep, coagulated red blotted out the white backdrop of his canvas, each fling of my wrist defining my masterpiece until my final stroke conjoined with his last breath and all that would be left of him was the crimson flow spilling messily onto the floor below.

Jason was a fool for picking Ivan and he should have known from my resulting silence that he had made a serious error. When he had decided to play a chord without my permission, I, the conductor, had left him to lead my orchestra on his own, and suddenly he could no longer hear the music, could not hear the murmurs of his colleagues, the divisions, the mutiny - his death.

I had warned him of his death many times before his betrayal, before I had stepped back into the shadows, leaving him in the spotlight. I had known how it would all end, simply based on his conduct. It wouldn't come quickly. He was my accomplice, the only person to stand beside me and witness the birth of Eclosion. He had to be careful in the decisions he made because so many looked to his guidance. He was too important; therefore, he wouldn't be graced with an assassination or a freak accident. No, fate would consume him slowly, like turning the dial on a stove from low to its highest setting, like a campfire gaining momentum as he added his own tinder to the flames.

I had told him, life has a sense of humor - no one dies but by their own weakness and choices. Distraction, greed, lust, anger - whatever the case, whatever drove them, consumed them. The ones who made decisions aimlessly, like my good friend Jason, always died metaphorically slow - these absent-minded individuals who heeded no warning. The people around them could see their deaths long before they happened. His type died before their time; they made idiotic mistakes at the expense of no one but themselves.

I had seen the writing on the wall, and in Jason's last moments, I had made his demise my advantage - to sustain the alibi that I had nothing to do with what I saw coming. I had told him to choose a better meeting place. I had told him not to advertise the location to employees, and I had demanded that he should lay low for a while, as naming an heir to the throne is as controversial as legalizing heroin. Publicly I had said this to him, for as a dissenter to his cause, I had seen that the factions needed to be mended, and besides, I had not wanted to see him get hurt. He was still our leader, for better or worse.

But he had disregarded my final words, as I had hoped he would, and now one headache had been alleviated. Now it was Ivan's turn to come to the plate, and I had just the right pitch.

"Are you okay?" my wife asked, breaking my concentration.

"Of course," I chuckled under my breath, "but I should probably get going."

"Without breakfast?"

"I'm going to have to."

"So...you don't know when you're coming back?"

"No clue, but I'll try to get back as soon as I can. I know your family will miss me."

"No meeting will take hours on Christmas Eve so don't go running off somewhere afterwards. Don't leave me alone like last time."

"I won't. I'll be back. Trust me," I recited by heart as I picked up our curious daughter who had happened to wobble into the kitchen, inspecting cracks in the tile floor. I gave her and my wife a quick kiss on the forehead and began gathering my coat and hat. Isabel bit her lip, as she usually does when her heart is hurting, her long hair blocking her wounded eyes, but I had no time for damage control.

"See you soon," I stated as I walked out of the kitchen, finally able to drop all acts and put on myself before I strolled out through the front door.

The drive to "headquarters," as our faithful followers christened it, was only about a ten-minute drive from my house, half an hour in traffic. It was a simple, inconspicuous building - a modest, heavily glass-windowed skyscraper that stood out like a blade of grass in rural Pennsylvania. To make ourselves even less obvious, the first fifteen floors were devoted solely to the insurance sector of our company. This worked wonderfully as some of our employees were former agents from the most well-known and prestigious insurance companies in the world. With their expertise, those fifteen floors alone generated enough profit to offset suspicion and ward off any inspectors that snooped around from time to time. It was a perfect front to take over the world - hiding in plain sight. After all, no one suspects insurance companies of crime, embezzlement, fraud, and corroding the well-being of our fellow man, right? Of course, even if someone did, what could they do about it?

The rest of the building housed Eclosion's secret agenda, complete with cubicles for each of our employees (to make them feel wanted), board rooms, halls for company events and even an indoor gymnasium complete with basketball courts, weight rooms, and an Olympic pool. Not to mention the fully loaded arcade, bowling alley and billiards hall. Needless to say, more of our plotting and scheming takes place over a best-out-of-three billiards match than in the board rooms. This was not just a revolution, it was a way of life, and we treated each other like family. If anything needed to be said to the company as a whole, there was a grand stage in place in which morning announcements and important speeches were given. This was the same stage in which Ivan gave his inauguration speech, wooing the crowd with an eloquence only the best of our writers could muster.

This was the same stage on which Jason and I had given several debates on the direction Eclosion should take in infiltrating society. It was also where we had received news of his death, which for me had been my last time on that stage. It held a bittersweet, nostalgic place in my memories, one I was determined to relive again someday. Ivan had made sure I wasn't to be involved in any of Eclosion's major activities, relinquishing my position and reducing me to clerical work – passing out bulks of mail (who writes letters anymore?), filling coffee cups and making sure the staff had time to do more important things. I hated my job. So much. Surely one could understand why Ivan must die.

This was why I was especially excited to hear that Ivan wanted to meet with me. Maybe he had had a change of heart and I could have my old job back and be the republican to his democrat. Or maybe (and this is the most likely notion), he decided to remove any unwanted contingencies in his plans. Either way, it was time for the sleeping giant to awake and feed once more.

When I got to headquarters, I expected business to go as usual – suit jackets and ties rushing in and out the building, calling up new clients to join our very real insurance agency...or the other one. I gave a casual wave here and there, employees eager to speak to me for no reason. To this day I can't understand why people are drawn to me.

One particular person, however, I tried to stay away from as much as possible, if for no other purpose than to stay off his radar. This individual was there to greet me in place of the usual doorman. Now, in order to talk to anyone about Eclosion's real activities, you had to pass through security. No one just walked into the real organization. You had to call the insurance company itself and be patched through to "customer service" after stating key words. After setting up an appointment for either that day or later (based on your rank in the company), you were able to come to "headquarters" with confirmation that you were cleared for entry. Every member had to be cleared whenever they entered the company, even me - even Ivan. The purpose was to not only catch any traitors, but to also keep any watchful eyes from suspecting us. Many people have gone "missing" over the years because they were "suspicious" as they talked with our employees before getting to Eclosion's private sector.

If you were finally cleared to enter the true "Eclosion," then you were escorted to your post or appointment. Who the escort was depended on your rank and purpose that day - the higher the importance of your appointment, the more dangerous the escort was. I was apprehensive the moment I saw mine this day, for it was not my usual escort, an ecstatic patriotic fellow named William Reins. This time, I was given the special treatment.

I had never met him personally, but his reputation arguably exceeded Ivan's. A man, known only by a title - Arcade – he was infamous for his propensity to play mind games with his colleagues. He would feign a good conversation, maybe even a friendship - until you slipped up and said the wrong thing, and you were never heard from again. He was an Eclosion operative to be feared and he had the power to carry out whatever he wanted, for he was none other than Ivan's right-hand man. No doubt Ivan had sent his bloodhound to sniff me out. I already knew I was on Ivan's radar, so I had taken precautions to avoid Arcade. Surely he noticed this, but never acted upon it until this "called meeting". If I was to get close to Ivan, I had no choice but to meet Arcade face-to-face...

"Vincent, my friend!" he exclaimed for the world to hear in a fake Australian accent. "How long it's been!"

"Hello," I said plainly, as I took note of all he decided to give me. I wondered what the unusual displays of body language meant, since he was surely a master of such things. Why were his hand gestures playing into the Italian stereotype? Did he come up with his casual, slightly slung-over standing posture? What could be said by the way he combed his hair, and the barely noticeable stubble that damped his tan skin? The clothing he wore - no logos, but would they have a brand name if I was to see the inside labeling? Was he sensitive about the scar on his left cheek? What caused it? Was it self-inflicted to paint the illusion that he had weaknesses?

Data was flooding my mind at a rate even I struggled to keep up with, but there was no time to process. The game had begun.

"I'm your escort," he said joyously. He was obviously excited for the hands in his pockets could barely stop shaking - his suit pants and jacket untamed in the excitement of running toward the door to greet me. I said nothing, only nodding as I walked ahead of him to the elevators. Arcade immediately slammed a hand to my chest to stop me. It didn't hurt, but the sudden movement momentarily caught me off guard.

"Uh-uh. Not that way. You go that way...it would have taken you straight to the castle."

I stared at him, trying to understand his words, but he only gave me a cheesy smile. He motioned me down a side hall and I obeyed for once in my life, walking leisurely with him.

"Not a movie buff, are you, Vincent?" he asked inquisitively.

"I don't have the time for it."

"Oh don't give me that, you have time. No one is a God here, and you need leisure time just like the rest of us. It's why men who do bad things eventually get caught, because at some point, they need to go to sleep, and then...they are as vulnerable as a baby."

"Sleep is a waste of time too," I said emotionlessly, "though necessary."

"Do you sleep well at night, Vincent?"

"I do."

"I believe you, and let me tell you why - because I think who you are - is not who you really are. Of course, everyone has a front - life's one big masquerade - but you, oh you win the prize for best costume. Your disguise takes some work, doesn't it? I'm sure it just wears you out at night. By the time you're done pretending, you're probably all puckered out, huh? Knocked out as soon as your head hits the pillow."

I said nothing but stared at him strangely.

"Look at me rambling on," Arcade chuckled. "I've always been too much of a talker. Come on, get onto the service elevator. It's right there to your left."

I risked insubordination, though I knew the answer already.

"Why? The personnel elevators are a lot faster, and they'll take no time getting to the top floor."

"So you know of the service elevator?"

"It's larger than the regular ones because of the cargo that has to be transported, most of it is fragile items - it's understandable why it's a lot slower. Not to mention it's old and hasn't been inspected in five years. This is common knowledge."

"True. True. Don't be so defensive next time. You're acting like every word I say is a test...which it is - but it's not, got it?"

"Yes."

"Good!" he said sharply, loud and awkward, forcing me out of my analytical stupor. His smile disappeared like lightning and a firm scowl emerged over his hideously freakish smile.

"We have much to discuss, Vincent. We must get to know each other."

He stared into my eyes, unmoved and focused. I played the coward and shifted my eyes down as he spoke. His eerie grin flashed back onto his face as he called the elevator down to our floor. I noticed it had started out at the top. A surprise party for me, perhaps? Arcade didn't let me dwell on the possibilities.

"How's the wife?" he asked innocently, though I kept my guard.

"Well. Very well."

"It sounds like you're describing your puppy's checkup at the vet. Why don't you tell me how she's really doing."

"She's hoping I get home in time to go to her parents. She wants me with the family – it being Christmas Eve and all."

"Yet any other day wouldn't matter, right? I heart traditions."

I tried to hold back my disgust at his use of the word "heart."

"It doesn't matter that I hate being at these family gatherings. She insisted I go. Still, I do it because I love her."

"She's your soulmate," Arcade said cheesily, swooning like was going to say "awww" at any second.

"I guess so."

"I don't believe in that kind of stuff," he said quickly. "Too mushy for me. I do believe in killmates though."

"Killmate?"

"You never heard of it? It's the same concept, with a little twist. It's the belief that there's two people in the world so completely disconnected in body and soul that if they should meet, all they want to do is kill each other. They simply have no choice in the matter. Same thing as soulmates, it's just they hate, not love."

I didn't know what to say to his offensive explanation. Arcade just smiled as the elevator dinged, announcing its arrival.

"Don't worry, Vincent. This will be painless, I promise."

I stepped on reluctantly, knowing that after the doors closed, there was no turning back. The service elevator was a little worn but functional, creaking the entire ride like something out of a bad horror movie. I noticed the floor was brand new; apparently Ivan and his men used it enough to lavish it with at least that.

I remained a statue as Arcade chuckled randomly, pressing the button to the top floor, the 55th. He held the button in for a long time and when he stepped away, the elevator began to climb, but at a crawl, taking a few minutes to reach the next floor. Obviously, there was a purpose to this. I could only imagine what it could be.

I kept my eye on Arcade who leaned up against a side wall and placed his hands in his suit pockets, his right leg placed gently over his left. He made sure to choose the only side with the floor buttons facing out, controlling any urge I might have to ditch our course. The smile on his face lost some of its warmth but he still kept it there as if to mask his true motives. He motioned for me to lean up against the opposite wall. I obeyed, ready for anything as he began the interrogation.

"Do you know why I like movies?" he asked. I allowed myself to laugh a little, for it was the same reason I loathed them.

"I have an idea."

"Have you heard of the biblical verse, 'there's nothing new under the sun?' It's my all-time favorite concept and I recite it every morning without fail. Do you know what it means?"

"Why don't you tell me?"

"You see, with that phrase in mind, I know I should have no fear of the unknown, because nothing is original. Nothing is new. It's why I like movies so much. No story line is ever original. It's exhilarating to be able to figure out the ending in the first ten minutes. I feel intelligent, superior almost, especially when others are still in shock when the credits roll. You see, I know that no matter how hard you try, everyone abides by formulas. Sure, an innovative film comes out once in a while and everyone is in an uproar over how insightful it is, but when you break it apart, you realize that there's nothing new or inventive about it at all. There's nothing original in this world - it's all been done before, and it applies to life and people as well. It's all routines and habits that have been learned and practiced over time, confined by our human limitations. No matter how tough someone acts, no matter how intelligent someone claims to be, there is a way to figure them out. You put up a good front, Vincent, but I've been watching you - and I like you, because you're good at hiding. You're that one movie I haven't figured out yet, and the film is playing out and I'm just getting more and more excited and angry and furious because I want to find out your secret before the film's over. I need to find out your secret. I know you have one - that much I've figured out. You're too protective of your extracurricular activities, too cautious, but I will win, because I've seen you before. There's nothing new under the sun! Nothing. There has been a person just like you on this earth. You're not immortal. If I were to attack you, I know for a fact that you have the same major organs and tendons and joints like everyone else. You have no more blood coursing through your veins than I do. You are capable of experiencing fear like I am, and pain, and yes, death. There is no difference between us. The only question is, who will slip up first?"

"Is this why I was called here? Because you suspect me of hurting the company? Ivan has confronted me before, and I haven't made any waves since."

"I know, Vincent - but honestly, I think you're just good at being cautious."

"What now?"

"Nothing. As you suspected, this is a test, but hey, do you know why I held in the button on the elevator?"

I scowled at Arcade's playful banter for he was testing me in ways I was not accustomed to. Usually when I met men who demanded to match wits, they were not ashamed to portray their superiority, which I loved, for in their over-confidence they usually made mistakes. I won't deny my own pride flares up at times but I try to keep it under control as much as possible. Arcade was testing the full extent of my patience, asking me erratic questions and spitting out philosophies that I was struggling not to respond to. I didn't know what lay for us on the 55th floor but it was apparent that the answers to Arcade's questions would determine my fate. He was asking at a rate that screamed urgency, though the questions themselves were ludicrous. It might be a good idea to stay silent but based on how frantic his questions were, remaining silent could result unfavorably. Maybe it was time to play Arcade's game on my own terms, and take the offensive.

"No. I have no clue why you held in the button, though I can speculate. The truth is I've never been on this elevator before."

This was true, since I had had to keep a low profile.

"The elevator will still reach its destination, but my holding in the button slowed the journey down to a crawl," he said, excited, marking a change in the tone of my voice.

"I've noticed."

"What's my name, Vincent? My real name?"

"What?" I had heard him, but I was unsure of his intentions.

"I asked you a question."

I studied his face carefully. He was serious, and he wanted an answer.

"I don't know your real name, nor do I see how this is relevant."

"You have no clue what my name is?"

"No. I-"

"I asked you a question! What's my name?!" Arcade practically screamed at me, still in the same position, but barely holding himself back, like a quivering rattlesnake poised to strike.

"Arcade, calm down. The fact is-"

"-What do you know about Ivan?!" he spat as he catapulted himself off of the wall, stopping just short of my face. The psychopath was trying to rustle my feathers but I gave him no leeway. Since playful conversation and intellectual exchange didn't get him the answers he wanted, he resorted to the only thing he truly knew: violence, the animal in him pushing humanity to the side as his questions resulted in no weight, no basis for conviction against me. Any answer I gave, no matter how ridiculous, was grounds for execution. This was the Arcade I had expected to eventually meet, the executioner, just not so early in the game. I had hoped to defeat him while he was in his more civilized manner.

"Ivan's our leader," I yelled back in his face, "and that's all I know. Not his name, his social security number, or what newspaper he likes to read when he's on the toilet. I know nothing! You hear me?!"

Sometimes, as degrading as it was, it was best to bark right back.

"You lay so low, Vincent, what are you planning?" he seethed as his face got closer to mine. I could smell the rotten odor of undercooked steak coating his breath. I got closer with no fear, for in his anger - as all angry men do - he was almost ready to strike, and despite my copy of his actions, I was in perfect complete control. He would make a move out of passion, which was always sloppy, and I would decapitate him with my logistical axe.

"I'm planning nothing," I stressed, but he refused to listen.

"WHAT ARE YOU PLANNING?!" he screamed in my face, shaking the elevator with his tempestuous fury.

"Nothing!!!" I shrieked back as he stepped forward.

A gun was placed to my head.

Don't miss out!

Visit the website below and you can sign up to receive emails whenever Julius St. Clair publishes a new book. There's no charge and no obligation.

https://books2read.com/r/B-A-MNLC-BTZWB

BOOKS 2 READ

Connecting independent readers to independent writers.

Also by Julius St. Clair

Angelic Testament
End of Angels
Angels of Eden
Angels and the Ark

Depression Series
Depression Vol 1

Fantasy World Earth Anthology
Fantasy World Earth Anthology Vol 1
Fantasy World Earth Anthology Vol 2

Fantasy World Naropa Anthology
Fantasy World: Naropa Anthology Vol 1
Fantasy World: Naropa Anthology Vol 2
Fantasy World: Naropa Anthology Vol 3

Fantasy World: The Explorers
Fantasy World
Fantasy World Vol 2 - Expedition One
Fantasy World Vol 3 - The Protectors
Fantasy World Vol 5 - Utopia

Julius St Clair Short Stories
Sanctuary (A Short Love Story)
My Best Friend is a Killer: Short Story Collection
World War Baby: Day One
World War Baby: Day Two
Static Rain
Girl of My Dreams
Face Punch
Face Punch II: Two for Flinching
Champion: Reluctant Hero
Champion #2: Family Reunion
Champion #3: Broken Promises
The Weather Brothers
The Weather Brothers #2: Fighting Immortals
The Weather Brothers Vs Champion
The First and Last Kiss

Sage Saga
The Last of the Sages
The Sage Academy (Book 1.5 of the Sage Saga)
The Dark Kingdom
Hail to the Queen

Of Heroes and Villains
The Legendary Warrior
The End of the Fantasy
Rise of the Sages
Ancient Knights
The Last War
The End of an Era
Hail to the King
The King's Apprentice
The Legend of the Sages

Sage Saga Bundle
The Sage Saga: The Complete Five Kingdoms Trilogy
The Sage Saga: The Complete Bastion Trilogy
The Sage Saga: The Complete Sorcerers Trilogy
The Sage Saga: The Complete Time Travel Trilogy

Sage Saga Collection
The Complete Sage Saga Collection
The Complete Sage Saga Collection Vol 2

Sage Saga Duologies
The Last of the Sages Book 1 and 2
The Last of the Sages Book 3 and 4
The Last of the Sages Book 5 and 6
The Last of the Sages Book 7 and 8
The Last of the Sages Book 9 and 10
The Last of the Sages Book 11 and 12

Seven Sorcerers Saga
The Sorcerer's Ring
The Sorcerer's Dragon
The Sorcerer's Blade
The Complete Seven Sorcerers Trilogy

The Rest Die Tomorrow Miniseries
The Rest Die Tomorrow - Ascension
The Rest Die Tomorrow - Judgment
The Rest Die Tomorrow - Killbox
The Rest Die Tomorrow - Endgame
The Rest Die Tomorrow: The Complete Collection
Shepherd of the Wolves

Wishes
A Wish for Love and Vengeance
A Wish for Us

Witchfall
The Harvest
The Blood Witch

Standalone
My Immortal Playlist

The Last of the Guardians
The End of Us